Come Home Bear
Written by Tommy Watkins

Mama Bear and her Cub walk down the road.

Storms land in the area with heavy rain and lightning!

The two bears run to safety, bu
the Mama Bear gets separated
from her Cub.

After the storm, the Cub is all alone, not knowing where to go.

Mama Bear looks everywhere for her Cub.

A woman driving on the road see the poor Cub lost.

Recognizing that the Mama Bear isn't with her Cub, she pulls over and tries to find Mama Bear.

The woman and the Cub walked for two hours. It seemed Mama Bear was nowhere to be found.

The moon started to rise in the sky, and a large shadow approached the woman and the Cub.

It was Mama Bear running to he
Cub! Mama Bear and the Cub
were reunited! She walked back
to her car with a smile, knowing
the Cub would be safe.

The End

Milton Keynes UK
Ingram Content Group UK Ltd.
UKHW051607250824
447237UK00017B/4